WOOF
AND THE
HAUNTED HOUSE

by Danae Dobson
Illustrated by Dee deRosa

WORD PUBLISHING
Dallas · London · Sydney · Singapore

To my best friend and lifelong companion, Kristin Marie.
Thank you for your devoted friendship,
for your support through difficult times,
and for sharing with me in many of life's adventures.
This story is dedicated to you.

Woof and the Haunted House

Copyright ©1989 by Danae Dobson for the text. Copyright ©1989 by Dee deRosa for the illustrations.
Scripture quotation is from *The Living Bible, Paraphrased,* copyright 1971 by Tyndale House Publishers,
Wheaton, IL. Used by permission.
Library of Congress Cataloging-in-Publication Data
Dobson, Danae.
Woof and the haunted house/by Danae Dobson: illustrated by Dee deRosa.
   p. cm.
   Summary: Influenced by local gossip about its former owner, three children have a terrifying experience
in a supposedly haunted house, but Jesus is there to protect them.
   ISBN 0-8499-8346-0:
   [1. Haunted houses — Fiction. 2. Christian life — Fiction.]
I. DeRosa, Dee, ill. II. Title.
PZ7.D6614Wp 1989
[E] — dc20   89-16623
Printed in the United States of America   CIP
9801239RA987654321   AC

A MESSAGE FROM
Dr. James Dobson

Before you read about this dog named Woof perhaps you would like to know how these books came to be written. When my children, Danae and Ryan, were young, I often told them stories at bedtime. Many of those tales were about pet animals who were loved by people like those in our own family. Later, I created more stories while driving the children to school in our car pool. The kids began to fall in love with these pets, even though they existed only in our minds. I found out just how much they loved these animals when I made the mistake of telling them a story in which one of their favorite pets died. There were so many tears I had to bring him back to life!

These tales made a special impression on Danae. At the age of twelve, she decided to write her own book about her favorite animal, Woof, and see if Word Publishers would like to print it. She did, and they did, and in the process she became the youngest author in Word's history. Now, ten years later, Danae has written five more, totally new adventures with Woof and the Petersons. And she is still Word's youngest author!

Danae has discovered a talent God has given her, and it all started with our family spending time together, talking about a dog and the two children who loved him. We hope that not only will you enjoy Woof's adventures but that you and your family will enjoy the time spent reading them together. Perhaps you also will discover a talent God has given you.

In the center of town, near Mark and Krissy Peterson's home, stood a spooky-looking house. Years ago it had belonged to a strange man whom people came to call Old Mr. Wilson. No one had known him very well, and he seemed to have no friends. Mr. Wilson looked funny, too. He had bent shoulders and long white hair, and he walked around town very slowly with the help of a big, black cane. Children were especially afraid of him in those years. They thought of him as a mysterious old man who lived in a scary house in the little city of Gladstone.

Mr. Wilson became even more strange as he grew older. He talked to

himself as he walked along the sidewalk, and he would sometimes stand in
his front yard for a long time, just looking into space. Of course, the children
in that part of town began to tell scary stories about the mysterious old man.

  As the years went by, Mr. Wilson began to be sick more often. Finally, as
he was about to have his eighty-sixth birthday, he went to bed one night,
and the Lord quietly took him to heaven. He had lived a very long life. The
next week a city workman came and boarded up the windows and doors so
that children would not go inside the old house. It was not a safe place to play!

All of this happened years before Mark and Krissy Peterson were born. By the time they came along, there was a great mystery in the town about Mr. Wilson's old house. Still, no one lived there. You would be surprised by the scary stories that were told about it by the school children. Parents sometimes let their kids believe the stories so they would stay away from the dark old house.

Mark, who was six years old, had heard all the tales. He wasn't sure he believed them, but the old place did look pretty scary. He walked past the Wilson house every afternoon on the way home from school. He would look at the lonely, dark building and wonder what it looked like inside.

"Someday," he thought, "I'll find out for myself!"

One Friday afternoon Mark decided this was the day. He hurried home from school to share his plan with his ten-year-old sister, Krissy. He ran through the front door and found her reading a book on the sofa.

"Krissy!" Mark exclaimed. "Listen! You know the old Wilson house on the next block?"

Krissy nodded.

"Let's go over there and explore the place!" Mark could tell by the look on his sister's face that she did not like the idea. "Come on, Krissy," he begged. "Let's go have a look."

Their dog, Woof, who had been lying in the corner on a blanket, sat up and cocked his head from side to side.

"I don't know, Mark," she said. "I'm afraid of that house. I've heard it's haunted and that a lot of strange things have gone on there."

Mark laughed at his sister. "That's silly. You're just a big coward. Please go with me. Besides, Mom won't let me go for a walk unless you come along."

Krissy thought for a moment. "Well, all right."

While Krissy went to get her jacket and a flashlight, Mark telephoned his best friend, Barney Martin, and asked him to join them. Barney agreed to go, and the two children and Woof began walking toward his house.

Barney met them at the front door, and he looked a little uneasy. He was obviously scared. "I decided not to go to the Wilson house," he said timidly. "It's too dangerous. My brother said he has heard all sorts of stories about weird things going on over there—things like people getting trapped and never getting out. He said some people have actually seen Old Man Wilson walking around the grounds and…"

"Stop it," Mark interrupted. "You're just being silly."

Woof barked and wagged his tail as if to agree.

Barney looked at the ground and put his hands in the pockets of his trousers. "Well, all right then, I'll go with you," he said, looking back up at his friends. "But if anything goes wrong, don't say I didn't warn you."

With that, the three children and Woof headed toward the old house. In a few minutes they could see the rooftop in the distance.

Barney froze when he caught sight of the house. "I don't want to go any further," he said nervously. "I'll just stay here and wait for you to come back . . . if you ever get back!"

Mark was beginning to lose patience with his friend. "Barney, would you stop being such a scaredy-cat and come on?" he said sternly.

Barney caught his breath and continued to walk, but he would have rather been anywhere than near the old house.

The children and Woof finally came to the entrance of the yard. Indeed it did look pretty frightening. Even Woof seemed a little uneasy as he sniffed the air. The children stood at the iron gate and gazed at the run-down house. It was surrounded by weeds and bushes. The windows and doors were nailed shut with boards that had been sloppily placed around the openings. The setting sun outlined the building with an orange glow as the trees swayed back and forth around its aging panels. Woof began to growl, and the hair stood up along his neck.

"Come on!" Mark said. "Let's see if we can find a way to get inside."

Krissy held her brother's arm as they crept slowly around the outside of the house. Woof trotted ahead of them and soon disappeared around the corner. In a second they heard him barking.

"Look! Woof found an opening!" Mark said excitedly as he rounded the corner.

Sure enough, a board had come loose from the side of the house.
"Let's go!" Mark exclaimed.
Barney gulped and held his breath as the three children and Woof pushed their way through the opening.

Inside, the house was dark, and the air was cold and musty-smelling. Mark turned on the flashlight and held it up high so they could see. So many mysterious shapes surrounded them! They stood listening to the wild beating of their hearts as they looked around the dusty old room. There were ancient pieces of furniture covered with sheets and a grandfather clock that was no longer ticking. In the corner stood Mr. Wilson's black cane, and on the table

lay a pair of tiny wire eyeglasses. Everything looked as though someone had left in a hurry.

The children stayed close together as they tiptoed across the creaky floor, being careful not to make too much noise.

"Hey! Look at this," Mark said, picking up a picture. "This must have been Mr. Wilson's wife." There in the frame was a photo of an older woman with white hair and a grandmotherly face.

The children continued searching the room—
looking at dusty books and admiring the antique furniture.
They had almost forgotten how frightened they had been when,
suddenly, Woof stiffened and growled. The hair on his back stood straight up!

Krissy grabbed her brother's arm tightly and gasped. "I'm scared!" she said.
"Me, too!" Mark admitted.

Barney was so frightened he couldn't say anything at all. He just stood
there with his teeth chattering and his knees knocking.

Before they decided what to do, Woof had already begun walking up the creaky staircase. As the three children clung to each other, Woof began making his way up the stairs, growling and sniffing the air. When he reached the second floor, he disappeared around the corner. In a few seconds, he began barking loudly.

"Let's go see what he's found," Mark whispered.

"No way!" Krissy said, shivering. "Let's get out of here!"

"Yeah!" Barney said with a tremble in his voice. "Let's go!"

"We can't just leave Woof up there, alone," Mark told them.

"But what if somebody is up there?" Krissy said with both hands over her face.

"We have to get Woof," Mark said. "He may be in trouble."

"Try to call him, Mark. Maybe he'll come," Barney suggested.

Mark went to the foot of the staircase and took a deep breath. "Woof. Come here, boy."

But Woof didn't come. He just continued to bark louder from a room at the top of the stairs.

"It's no use," Mark said firmly. "We have to go up there and get our dog. Besides, I want to know why he's barking."

The three children joined hands and huddled close together. Carefully they made their way up the rickety stairs that squeaked with every step. Mark, in the lead, held firmly to the flashlight.

Suddenly, Krissy screamed!
One of the old boards had given way, trapping
her foot inside the step. "Help me!" she cried.
Mark grabbed her by the hand. "It's all right," he assured her.
"We'll get you out."

After several tugs Mark and Barney managed to loosen Krissy's foot from
the hollow staircase. Tears were streaming down her face, but she had only
scraped her ankle.

Soon the children started up the stairs again. This time they were more
cautious about where they stepped. When they reached the top, Mark aimed
the flashlight down the dark hallway. They could still hear Woof barking
in one of the rooms.

"It looks pretty creepy," Mark said.

"Why did I agree to come here anyway?" Barney mumbled to himself.

Slowly the children began tiptoing down the hallway in the direction of their barking dog.

"Here boy," Mark called. He called again, but Woof just kept on barking and growling.

Finally the children reached the room where Woof was. Their hearts pounded like big bass drums as they peered inside, ready to run for safety at any moment. Woof was barking angrily at the closet door.

Krissy grabbed her brother's arm again. "Something is in that closet!" she exclaimed.

Barney was shaking so much he could barely keep his balance. "What could be in there?" he whispered.

Suddenly, a gigantic crash came from inside the closet, and the door flew open! All three children screamed and jumped in the air at the same time. Then they turned and ran toward the stairs.

"Get me out of here!" Barney shouted.

Even though the children were running as fast as their legs would carry them, it wasn't fast enough to escape from what was behind them. In just a few seconds, a big, yellow cat came tearing past them on the stairs and darted out the opening with Woof hot on his tail. Three kids and a dog scrambled for the opening, all trying to get out at the same time.

Then they ran like the wind down Pine Street with Barney leading the way. The yellow cat headed off in another direction and climbed the nearest tree. Their hearts were beating wildly and sweat was dripping from their faces as they reached the driveway of the Peterson home.

Mr. and Mrs. Peterson were startled as the three children and Woof came running through the front door. They knew by the look on the children's faces that something was wrong. Everyone began talking at once as the children tried to explain what had happened.

"Wait a minute," Father interrupted. "One at a time, please."

Mark began by telling how the Wilson house was haunted. Krissy and Barney told about the loud noise and the strange cat they had seen. Even Woof was barking as loud as he could.

After the children were finished, Mr. Peterson called two neighbors to go with him to investigate the old house. While they were gone, Mother tried to comfort the children, who were still very upset. Woof seemed just as uneasy as he lay on his blanket whimpering softly.

An hour later Mr. Peterson returned. The children jumped up and met him at the door.

"Well," Mark asked. "What happened?"

Mr. Peterson smiled and said, "I think we solved the mystery of the haunted house. Let's sit down, and I'll tell you about it."

The children sat on the edge of their seats and listened closely as Father began.

"It would seem that a big, yellow cat was snooping around the house and became trapped in the closet somehow. Woof's barking must have frightened him because it appears that he knocked over a stack of dusty boxes left by Mr. Wilson. That's what caused the loud crash you heard. When the boxes fell, they hit the door and made it fly open. That's when the three of you became so frightened. Woof chased the cat out of the house, and he darted up a nearby elm tree, where we found him."

The children were greatly relieved. "I'm so glad the house isn't really haunted like everyone says," Krissy said.

"Me, too," Barney added. "I thought we were all going to die in there."

Everyone laughed about how frightened they had been on account of a cat.

"Now wait a minute," Father said. "I hope you kids learned a valuable lesson from this experience. Exploring that old house was not smart. Someone could have gotten hurt. Krissy was fortunate that her accident on the staircase wasn't worse than it was." The children nodded in agreement.

"We know what we did was wrong," Mark added. "But we're thankful that Jesus protected us anyway."

The next morning Mr. Peterson took the children to a museum, a place where old things are kept. While they were there, they looked at old pictures and read books about Mr. Wilson. They learned many interesting things about him—things that were different from the bad stories they had heard. Mr. Davis, the man who worked at the museum, told them that Mr. Wilson had been a very good man. He had given away lots of money to help others.

Mark and Krissy were amazed at what they had learned about Mr. Wilson. "Then none of those awful stories were true?" asked Krissy.

Father nodded. "That's right. Mr. Wilson was a fine Christian gentleman. He just lived longer than his family and friends, and the loneliness and his old age made him seem much different than he really was."

Later that day when the Petersons had returned from the museum, Father got out the Bible and turned to the book of James. Mark and Krissy sat beside him on the couch and listened as he taught them an important lesson.

"You see, children," he began, "gossip can be a dangerous thing. Many people have been hurt by stories told about them that weren't true. In James

chapter 3 we read: 'If anyone can control his tongue, it proves that he has perfect control over himself in every other way.'" Father continued, " 'So also the tongue is a small thing, but what enormous damage it can do.' "

"Just like with Mr. Wilson," Krissy said. "Someone made up a scary story about him and his house, and soon the whole town believed it."

"That's right," Mr. Peterson said. "We should always be careful not to believe rumors, and we should not repeat them to others."

"I'm sure I would have liked Mr. Wilson if I had known him," Mark said.

"Me too," Krissy agreed. "He wasn't at all like I heard."

"He might have even liked Woof," said Mark, stroking the hair on his dog's head.

Mr. Peterson smiled. "He probably would have," he said thoughtfully. "In fact, I'm sure he would have. Doesn't everybody?"